THE ADVENTURES OF MERM, THE CAT

WRITTEN & ILLUSTRATED
BY CHELSEA POHL

" THE ADVENTURES OF MERM, THE CAT"
IS A PUBLICATION OF MYRIAD BOOK PUBLISHING LLC.

101 2ND AVE #309 DES MOINES, IA 50309
WWW.MYRIADPUBLISHING.COM - 515.418.2000

FOR
SANNY BEES

MERM WAS
A VERY SPECIAL
CAT.

HE LOVED
TO EAT.

HE LOVED
TO SLEEP.

AND
OCCASIONALLY
HE LIKED TO READ
A GOOD BOOK.

MERM WAS ALSO
THE FRIENDLIEST
CAT IN THE
WHOLE WORLD.

HE GOT TO
TRAVEL ALL OVER
THE WORLD ON
A BOAT WITH
HIS FAMILY.

DURING THEIR TRAVELS,
THE LITTLE GIRLS IN THE
FAMILY HEARD SO MANY NEW
LANGUAGES THAT THEY BEGAN
TO SPEAK ONE OF THEIR OWN.
THEY CALLED IT "MERMER
TALK," IN HONOR OF THEIR
VERY SPECIAL CAT.

MERMER TALK
QUICKLY SPREAD
ALL OVER
THE WORLD.

An opera was
even inspired by
the new language.
It was called,
"The Mermer Talk
Opera."

Merm became famous. Everyone wanted to meet the cat that inspired a new language.

He met
kings and queens,
presidents and
prime ministers.

HE WAS EVEN INTERVIEWED ON TV!

Everyone wanted to know what the key to Merm's success was. So, he decided to write an advice book, which was really quite simple. All it said was, "Eat well. Sleep well, and occasionally read a good book. – Merm"

To order
or for more info about
"The Adventures of Merm the Cat"

Go to MYRIADPUBLISHING.COM
or contact J. Brommel at
515.418.2000

LaVergne, TN USA
13 November 2010
204753LV00002B

9781450725026